Where Do Diggers Trick-or-Treat?

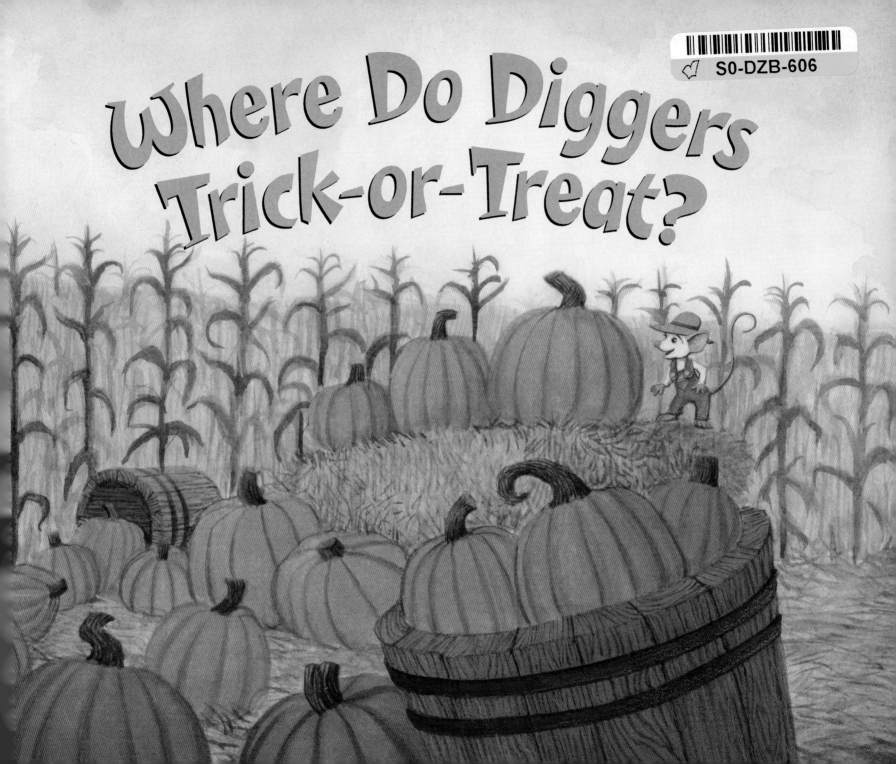

Visit us on the Web! rhcbooks.com

Educators and librarians, for a variety of teaching tools, visit us at RHTeachersLibrarians.com

Library of Congress Cataloging-in-Publication Data is available upon request.
ISBN 978-0-593-31017-5 (board) — ISBN 978-0-593-31018-2 (ebook)
ISBN 978-0-593-64770-7 (pbk.)

MANUFACTURED IN CHINA
10 9 8 7 6 5 4 3 2

First Dragonfly Books Edition 2023

Where Do Diggers Trick-or-Treat?

by Brianna Caplan Sayres · illustrated by Christian Slade

Dragonfly Books ——✦ New York

Where do diggers trick-or-treat
after digging giant holes?
Do they fill their scoops with chocolate treats—
like enormous candy bowls?

Where do tractors trick-or-treat
after chores in early morn?
Does a pumpkin patch await them
through a zigzag maze of corn?

Where do recycling trucks trick-or-treat
after cardboard fills their tummies?
Does a roll of toilet paper
help them become recycling mummies?

Where do road rollers trick-or-treat
after helping make roads wider?
Do they squeeze the autumn apples
to make steaming apple cider?

Where do cranes trick-or-treat
after hoisting things up high?
Do they raise a ghastly ghost
to fly across the moonlit sky?

Where do monster trucks trick-or-treat
after leaping through the air?
They don't need to put on costumes.
They're already dressed to scare!

Where do drill rigs trick-or-treat
after drilling on a hill?
Do they drill a truck-o'-lantern
to put on the windowsill?

Where do flatbeds trick-or-treat
after moving wood and steel?
Do they haul a creepy castle
as a haunted-house-mobile?

Are there spiderwebs and candy corn
and a scarecrow, maybe two?
Is there spooky Halloween music
and little trucks that shout out "Boo"?

Where do your trucks trick-or-treat?
They can't wait for candy sharing!
When the doorbell rings—surprise!—
see the costumes they are wearing!

Getting to dreamland has never been more fun!

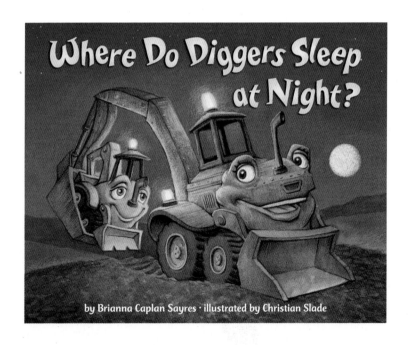

Where Do Diggers Sleep at Night?

by Brianna Caplan Sayres · illustrated by Christian Slade

Where Do Diggers Say I Love You?

by Brianna Caplan Sayres · illustrated by Christian Slade

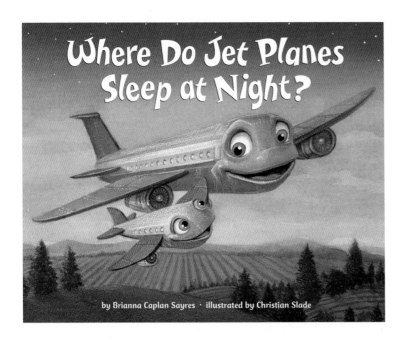

Where Do Jet Planes Sleep at Night?

by Brianna Caplan Sayres · illustrated by Christian Slade

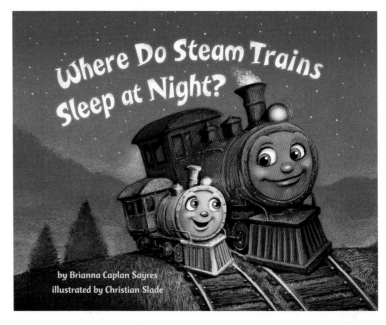

Where Do Steam Trains Sleep at Night?

by Brianna Caplan Sayres
illustrated by Christian Slade

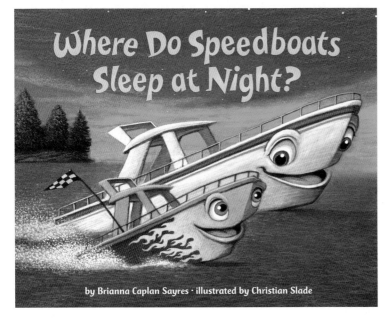

Where Do Speedboats Sleep at Night?

by Brianna Caplan Sayres · illustrated by Christian Slade

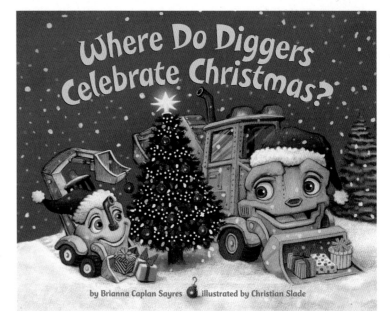

Where Do Diggers Celebrate Christmas?

by Brianna Caplan Sayres · illustrated by Christian Slade

Brianna Caplan Sayres

used to tell her second graders, "When I grow up, I'm going to be a writer."

"But you are grown up, Mrs. Sayres," her students would protest.

Well, Brianna is still not quite sure she's grown up, but she has grown into a writer. She is proud to be the author of the bestselling Where Do . . . book series, all illustrated by Christian Slade. Brianna lives with her husband and their two boys in Seattle.

Visit her on the web at briannacaplansayres.com and on Facebook at @authorbrianna.

Christian Slade

loves everything about being an artist. His distinctive art style can be found in picture books, novels, and magazines for children, and even on ice cream containers, among other wacky places! He received his BFA in drawing and animation from the University of Central Florida and his MA in illustration from Syracuse University. He lives with his wife and two children in Florida.

Visit him on the web at christianslade.com.